# The Piano

by Edgar J. Hyde

Illustrations by Chloe Tyler

PAB-0608-0300 • ISBN: 978-1-4867-1876-4

Copyright ©2020 Flowerpot Press, a Division of Flowerpot Children's Press, Inc., Oakville, ON, Canada.

Printed and bound in the U.S.A.

# Table of Contents

# CHAPTER ONE

## A Stroke of Luck

Roger Houston checked his mirror, turned on his blinker, and brought the car to a stop on the side of the road. His wife, beside him, yawned and stretched.

"Where are we?" she asked sleepily.

"Somewhere named Granville. Isn't it nice?" he replied. "I think I may fall asleep at the wheel if I don't get out for awhile and stretch my legs. We better wake up the children."

The Houston family was returning from their annual Easter trip and had been driving since early that morning. Mr. Houston felt his eyes ache with the strain of driving for so long and felt the need for some refreshment.

Granville, thought Mr. Houston, looks like the perfect place to stop and have lunch.

The children, roused from sleep by their mother, were rubbing their eyes, stretching wearily, and getting ready to get out of the car.

"Don't forget your jacket, Victoria. It's colder than you think," said Mrs. Houston. "You too, Darren, where's your jacket?"

Mrs. Houston busied herself getting the children ready while her husband leaned against the outside of the car, enjoying the fresh air.

"Nice place. This really is picturesque," he said to no one in particular. "I can't believe we've never noticed it before."

His thoughts were interrupted by his family spilling noisily out onto the pavement. Darren's hair, as it typically did, stuck up in all different directions, while he could see his practically-a-teenager daughter check her reflection in the car's side mirror and smooth down her hair before making sure her metallic blue nail polish wasn't chipped.

"Dad, Mom, can we go to the toy store? Can we, please, please?" Darren bounced up and down, looking eagerly from one parent to the other as he waited for his parents to answer. Mr. Houston shook his head sternly.

"Listen, young man," he told his six-year-old son, "we have enough new toys packed in the trunk of the car without buying anymore. I'm surprised the car was able to move at all with all that weight in the back."

Darren looked momentarily crestfallen then, brightening, took his dad's hand and asked, "Can I buy some candy then, Dad, can I, please? I have five dollars left in my pocket, please."

Grabbing his son's small, sticky hand—what has that child been eating now, he thought to himself—Mr. Houston turned left onto a small side street before muttering absentmindedly, "Depends on whether or not you eat your lunch, son."

Mrs. Houston and Victoria walked behind
more leisurely—Mrs. Houston admiring the pretty
flower boxes adorning the fronts of the small, white
houses, Victoria looking hopefully for a beauty
store. As they turned onto the side street, they
found Mr. Houston and Darren, noses pressed hard
against a shop window. Looking up, Mrs. Houston
noticed the sign above the store: Larkspur Music.
She and her daughter joined the others, and they
too pressed their noses against the window to see
the instruments stored inside. Though everything
looked pretty dusty, the family was thrilled to see a
range of musical instruments: a cello, some violins,
guitars, a huge drum kit that took up most of the left
side of the window, and much more.

"Let's go in," Mrs. Houston said, glancing at the
open sign on the front of the door. Though neither
she nor her husband had any musical skills to speak
of, Mrs. Houston had always wanted to be able to

play something.

Pushing open the door, the family entered the shop and there, right in the center, stood the most beautiful piano they had ever seen. Predominantly white, it stood proudly with its lid open, showing polished keys that seemed to simply cry out for someone to play them. Victoria, three years into piano lessons, was the first to run her fingers along the keys.

"Oh, Mom, Dad, it's perfect—can we buy it, please?"

Mr. Houston was aghast. "Buy it, Victoria? You can't be serious. Do you know how much these things cost? Put the lid down, you're not supposed to touch, you know."

"Don't be so hard on her, dear," Mrs. Houston intervened. "I can understand how she feels. It really is beautiful."

She too moved closer to the piano and ran her own fingers along the keys. As a child, Mrs. Houston had hoped her parents would send her to piano lessons, but unfortunately, the money was always needed elsewhere, and she had never fulfilled her dream.

"Can I help you?" came a voice from the far end of the store. An elderly man was walking toward them. "Ah, you've taken a liking to the piano, have you, my dear?" He smiled at Victoria.

"Well, yes, it is so beautiful," she said. "I didn't mean to touch it, really, I just couldn't help myself."

"Oh, don't worry about that," he returned. "Most people who come in here are drawn to the piano. Have a seat. What about you, young man? Would you like to sit on the stool alongside your sister?"

Darren was seated on the stool almost before the words had left the owner's mouth. His sister, seated half on and half off, grimaced at her brother before gently touching the keys while Darren, brasher than Victoria, began to roughly play his scales.

"Would you be interested in buying, sir, madam?"

The man smiled at them both. "I'm quite sure you'll be surprised at the price."

Mrs. Houston had no doubt about that whatsoever!

"$400," the owner was saying. "And we'll deliver it to you, free of charge."

Dad smiled. The old guy must be under the impression they want to buy the stool!

"Now what on earth would be the point in having a stool with no piano?"

"$400?" Mrs. Houston turned quizzically to the man. "Does that include the stool?"

Though disbelieving of the price, she wasn't one to waste an opportunity!

"Yes, of course, madam. The piano, the stool, and delivery. We can get it to you by, say, Monday morning." Checking the wall calendar quickly, he nodded in confirmation. "Yes, Monday should be fine. Now, if you'd just give me your address, we'll fill out the form. Tedious, all the forms you have to complete these days."

And just like that, the piano belonged to the Houston family. Dad left the shop in a complete daze, having filled in and signed a check for $400, given his name, address, and phone number to the owner, and stuffed a receipt in his wallet.

"Oh, don't look like that, Roger," said Mrs. Houston. "It's such a stroke of luck, finding an instrument in that condition, and at that price."

Taking both her children by the hand, she strode off in front of her husband, leaving him to shake his head over the events that had just taken place.

# CHAPTER TWO

## Strange Music

"Here comes the truck now!" shouted Darren from upstairs.

He had been keeping watch since eight that morning, excited about the delivery of the piano, and now could hardly contain himself. Throwing himself down the stairs, he was the first to the front door, almost tripping over a stray skate.

The truck pulled up outside the house and two men got out, made their way to the back of the truck, and unlocked the doors. Mr. Houston by now had appeared outside, and he directed the men to put the piano into the large room that was used partially for storage and partially for the children's toys. Everything in the room had been frantically pushed to one side that morning in order to make room for the family's new prized possession. Mr. Houston paid the men a little something extra, thanked them graciously, and shut the door, shaking his head disbelievingly; he had truly never believed the family would ever see the piano again.

"Let me sit down! Let me sit down!" shouted Darren, as both children tried to push themselves onto the piano stool.

"It's not big enough for both of us," his older sister replied. "Get off—it's my turn first—you can't even play piano."

"Now, now," Mrs. Houston intervened, "no fighting. What we'll do is have one hour for Victoria followed by one hour for Darren. Victoria first. Darren, come over here beside me and let your sister play."

Turning to her daughter, she continued, "And since you know so much more about the piano than

Darren does, why don't you try and help him? Let's be constructive instead of arguing with one another."

Victoria shrugged and turned her full attention to the gleaming keys, while Darren stared at the clock, willing the next hour to pass quickly.

And so the day passed, with both parents being aware of scales being practiced, hearing the odd notes of "Chopsticks," intermingled with the children having the occasional argument. At the end of the night, everyone climbed wearily into bed and fell fast asleep.

𝄞            𝄞            𝄞

Mr. Houston was the first one to wake up the next morning. He looked at his alarm clock—7:30 a.m.! He nudged his wife.

"Emily? Do you hear that?"

Reluctantly she turned to face him. "What is it dear? I'm sleepy."

Then, realizing her husband was sitting up in bed, she rubbed her eyes and sat up too. It was only then that she became aware of the strange and beautiful music drifting upstairs.

"Listen," said her husband. "Can you hear it now? Come on, let's go downstairs. I didn't realize Victoria was so accomplished."

The parents both made their way to the top of the stairs and began their descent. The music still played, a haunting melody, which neither of them seemed to have heard before. They went down the stairs quietly, not wanting to disturb Victoria, and somehow unwilling to cut into the perfection of the music.

As they reached the last stair and rounded the hallway leading to the room that housed the piano, Mr. Houston stopped and gasped. He could see, in the far corner of the room, Victoria shuddering!

"Victoria! What's going on? It can't possibly be Darren playing, can it?"

As both parents ran into the room, they were aware of their small son joining them from behind.

"Why is everybody up so early?" he was

mumbling. "What's going on?"

His parents and sister did not answer, and as he followed their gaze, he realized why. The piano was playing itself!

Victoria seemed very frightened, she being the one who had first heard the music and the first one downstairs. Mrs. Houston reached out to pull her close. She was also very shaken by what she saw, and as the whole family looked on, the piano continued to play, changing tempo, getting faster and faster, louder and louder, making a great thumping sound which threatened to wake the whole neighborhood. The beautiful strains of music they had heard from upstairs now seemed angry and frenzied, and the family could do nothing but wait until the piano eventually fell silent.

The family too was silent, shocked, and stunned by what they had all just witnessed. Victoria was visibly shaking and her mother had turned a ghastly shade of white. Mr. Houston was the first to speak.

"Well, what on earth was all that about?" he said, sitting down on the nearest chair and pulling Darren onto his knee.

"Oh no, I didn't want it to stop!" said Darren. "That was fun!"

"Fun?" echoed Victoria. "Don't be ridiculous. It was terrifying! How did it play its own keys? No one was touching it. It's not one of those windup ones, is it, Mom? You know, the kind you turn the key and the piano plays certain songs?" She looked at her mom hopefully.

"I don't think so," replied Mrs. Houston, and even though before she had been pretty sure this wasn't the case, she decided to go and look. She and Victoria checked everywhere they could think of— underneath, on top, behind, even the pedals for any clues as to what might have just happened.

"Nothing there, I'm afraid," said Mrs. Houston, finally giving up.

The family sat around in silence, each with their

own thoughts.

No wonder it was such a bargain, Mr. Houston was thinking to himself. It must be haunted or something. Just as the thought entered his head, he dismissed it, reminding himself he didn't believe in ghosts!

The ringing of the doorbell shook them again. Darren jumped up from his dad's knee and ran toward the front door to see who it was. It was Simon from two doors down.

"Hey, Darren, didn't know if you were back or not. Are you going back to school today?"

Mr. Houston looked at his watch. Ten minutes until 8 a.m.! What on earth was Simon doing at the front door over an hour before school!

Victoria reluctantly got to her feet.

"I guess I better start getting ready for school, too. What a weird start to the day," she yawned as she started to climb the stairs.

Mr. and Mrs. Houston looked at each other.

"Well, do you have any explanation?" Mrs. Houston asked.

Mr. Houston looked thoughtfully at the piano. "Trick of the light? We imagined the whole thing? Who on earth knows? Let's go get some breakfast. I think better on a full stomach."

# CHAPTER THREE

## A Death in the Family

Mrs. Houston put the telephone down and plopped down with a sigh.

"What's wrong, dear?" asked Mr. Houston, looking up from his newspaper.

"That was the woman from the nursing home. Auntie Maude died."

"I didn't know Auntie Maude was sick," said Darren, between mouthfuls of breakfast cereal.

"She wasn't really sick, sweetie, just old and tired, I suppose. She was ninety-three, you know." She turned toward Mr. Houston. "The funeral's tomorrow. The woman was unable to reach me, obviously, since we were on vacation. I know you won't be able to make it, but I'll go. There won't be many people there, I would think, and anyway, I'd like to pay my respects. I know we weren't close, but she was family." She smiled at the children. "Come on, you two, hurry up and finish breakfast, or you'll be late for school. And remember, Victoria, piano lessons right after school. Your first recital must be coming up soon, isn't it?"

"Yes," replied her daughter. "Next week, actually. I'm not worried, though. Miss Stewart says that if I can play "Für Elise" at the recital as well as I play it in practice, I'll be just fine."

"Stay sharp, young lady," said Mr. Houston, folding his newspaper and draining the contents of his cup. "You can never practice too much."

Turning to kiss his wife goodbye, he did not see his daughter roll her eyes then stick her tongue out in the direction of her younger brother, who sat watching her.

Victoria jumped down from the table, grabbed

her backpack and walked toward the door.

"Catch you later," she shouted over her shoulder. She blew Darren a kiss. "Bye, sweetie," she mimicked their mom, and ran out of the door before Darren could take aim with his spoon.

"Ugh! Sisters!" he exclaimed. I'll get her back tonight, he thought. As he ate the rest of his breakfast, he plotted how to annoy her when she got home.

After Mr. Houston left, Mrs. Houston cleared away the breakfast dishes while Darren peeked at what she had put in his backpack for his morning snack and thought about the story he was going to tell Simon.

"Ten minutes until nine," Mrs. Houston said, looking at the clock. "Better go!"

Darren was still too young to walk to school on his own, so his mom drove him there and picked him up in the afternoons.

Next year, maybe, he thought, looking enviously

at some older boys walking on their own.

♪     ♪     ♪

Mrs. Houston had a busy day, catching up with all the laundry from vacation and getting the house in order. She looked around the rooms fondly.

She wasn't sure that she wanted to move, though Mr. Houston seemed to have his heart firmly set on buying the old house on top of the hill. They had gone to see it just before setting off on vacation, and although she admitted there was a certain charm about the old place, she just didn't know if she was ready to leave her home. The children had always lived here, their friends were here, and both their schools were great and within walking distance.

"They'll meet new friends when we move," Mr. Houston had said, "and maybe they can still go to the same schools—there are buses they can catch after all."

Mrs. Houston sighed. The new house was beautiful, she supposed, and the yard was much bigger than the one they had now.

The older gentleman who lived there had a sun room added on only a few years ago. Wheelchair bound, this was where he spent his days looking out over his beloved garden. Mr. and Mrs. Houston had both agreed that this room, full of sunlight, would be perfect for the children's playroom.

The old man's daughter had only recently persuaded him to live with her, and so the house had been put up for sale. Mr. Houston had been so excited.

"It's within our price range, dear," he said when Mrs. Houston had expressed doubt, and she still felt the same doubt.

She seemed unable to shake the feeling as she went from room to room, picking up discarded items of clothing from Victoria's bedroom and rescuing the suspended "bungee jumping" doll from inside Darren's window. Smoothing out the little doll's dress, she put her back in Victoria's bedroom making a mental note to tell Darren that while bungee jumping was all right for his toy soldiers, it wasn't really suitable for his sister's elegant dolls.

Going into the children's playroom, Mrs. Houston ran her duster over the piano keys. The notes played as she touched them, but there was no repeat performance of the playing that had taken place earlier.

Maybe they had imagined it, she thought to herself, as she polished the top of the piano. After all, how can a piano play on its own? We were all probably tired from the long drive back.

She closed the lid, pushed in the piano stool, and left the room.

Now, she thought, is my black suit okay to wear to the funeral?

Shaking out the duster, she climbed the stairs to her bedroom to examine the contents of her closet.

# CHAPTER FOUR

## Discipline

"Good, Victoria. That was quite good." Miss Stewart nodded, as her young student finished playing. "Now, do you want to schedule another practice before your recital next Tuesday?"

"Thank you for the offer, Miss Stewart." The young girl smiled as she got up and said, "But my mom and dad just bought a new piano, so now I'll be able to practice whenever I want."

"Did they really, dear? Well isn't that just marvelous. I do hope you put it to good use, Victoria. You have talent, you know, but you must remember the key word..."

Discipline, remembered Victoria.

"...discipline," said Miss Stewart, right on cue. "You must discipline yourself if you want to be a really good pianist."

Victoria, her back toward her teacher, mouthed the words in perfect timing with Miss Stewart. Though she was a good teacher, and Victoria liked her, her use of the word discipline could be exhausting at times. Folding her music sheets and placing them inside her folder, Victoria nodded as Miss Stewart droned on and on.

"I had a student once, way before your time, who could have made something of herself. Extremely talented and a real pleasure to teach. Then she lost interest, you see, as she progressed. She found it was becoming more like work, and she simply didn't have the discipline to see it through."

Victoria stared hard at her shoes. Honestly, if she had to listen to this story one more time, she thought she'd scream. Next she'd get the lecture about being interested in boys and not bothering to show up for lessons.

"Of course, the next thing you know, she's not bothering to show up for lessons, choosing instead to 'hang out' with friends and making eyes at the young men who walked by."

Pointedly pulling up her sleeve to look at her watch, Victoria grabbed her bag and turned toward the door.

"Miss Stewart, I'm sorry, I really don't mean to interrupt, but I have to go. I promised my mom I'd help her clean the playroom tonight. Sorry, I'll see you next week!"

"Oh, right, bye then, dear."

From where she now sat on the sofa, Miss Stewart removed her glasses and rubbed her eyes.

"Half an hour until my next student," she observed, looking at the clock on the mantelpiece. "Think I'll just have a little nap while I wait."

And, placing her feet on the little stool in front of her, she pulled her cardigan around her shoulders and fell fast asleep.

♪          ♪          ♪

Later that night, when dinner was over and the last of the children's toys had been boxed in the playroom, Mr. Houston suggested that Victoria play "Für Elise" for them.

Settling herself on the piano stool, Victoria began to play. At first she faltered a little, then, as she grew in confidence, the notes flowed perfectly from beneath her fingers.

Mr. Houston sat back in his chair and closed his eyes. Isn't that beautiful, he thought to himself, pleased after all that they had bought the piano.

Then, suddenly, the haunting melody changed pace. The notes coming from the piano became louder and faster, and as Mr. Houston opened his eyes and sat forward in his chair, he saw that his daughter was no longer playing the instrument but had recoiled back in fear, her fingers suspended in midair. Darren was jumping up and down excitedly.

"It's doing it again! It's doing it again!" he screamed.

Mrs. Houston was on her feet and making her way toward her daughter. She put her arm around the girl's shoulders and stared, entranced, at the keys.

The piano seemed to have a mind entirely of its own, and the family noticed after a while that it played the same song over and over, only sometimes more quickly and more angrily than others. Eventually the playing stopped, and both parents turned to look at one another.

"Imagination? Trick of the light?" said Mr. Houston.

"I don't think so, somehow. There's something strange happening here, and we have to find out what it is," said Mrs. Houston.

# CHAPTER FIVE

## The Ancient Oak

Mrs. Houston shook hands with the rosy-cheeked woman standing before her.

"She was a lovely old soul, really she was. Brought joy to a lot of people, she truly did. She loved to sing and always sang a little something at the monthly concerts we had in the home."

Mrs. Houston smiled at the woman.

"Yes," she agreed. "I remember her singing. When I was much younger, my father used to take me to visit Auntie Maude and sometimes she would sing—only because he asked her, of course, because as you know, she wasn't one to brag about things."

The two spoke fondly of the old lady, then when

they heard the organist begin to play inside the little chapel attached to the crematorium, they made their way inside.

I was right about the amount of people attending, thought Mrs. Houston as she took off her gloves and took a seat.

Apart from herself, the woman from the nursing home, and the chaplain, there were only three other people in the chapel. It wasn't that Maude hadn't been liked, she thought to herself, it was just that all the friends she had were either dead or too frail and ill to attend the service.

There was a hymn first, then the chaplain said a few words about Maude and how kind she was. When he'd finished speaking, the organist began to play as the coffin moved out of sight behind the black velvet drapes.

That's the same song, thought Mrs. Houston in disbelief. It's exactly the same song as the one the piano's been playing at home! She glanced at the organist, but her face was impassive as she played each note.

Looking down at the funeral program, which had been given to her when she entered the chapel, she scanned it quickly.

Hymn: "The Lord Is My Shepherd"
Blessing: Chaplain Christopher Blount
Organ Solo: "The Ancient Oak" by Jessica Perry

She stopped reading. Jessica Perry. She knew that name. It had seemed familiar immediately, but why?

People were standing, she noticed, as the final hymn was being sung. She pushed the program into her bag and joined the others in song.

It wasn't until she was stopped at a traffic light on the way home that she remembered. Of course, Jessica Perry. Nurse Jessica Perry. She had been the midwife who had helped deliver Victoria over twelve years ago, and she was a piano teacher, too.

Mrs. Houston remembered her well. Almost the same age as herself, Nurse Perry had been with her throughout what had been a particularly difficult birth and seemed to take almost as much delight in the newborn, red-faced, screaming child as the proud parents themselves. She had visited mother and daughter every day for each of the eight days they spent in hospital—Mrs. Houston having developed a throat infection and baby Victoria a bad case of jaundice.

Shaken from her reverie by the sound of a car horn blaring behind her, Mrs. Houston noticed the light had changed to green and pushed the gas.

She didn't know Jessica had published any music, but then why would she? They had lost touch over eight years ago when Jessica had transferred to another hospital and left the district.

Mrs. Houston wondered if she had ever married. She knew Jessica had wanted children of her own, and that she had been very fond of Victoria, visiting whenever she could and never forgetting a birthday. It had been Jessica who had given the little girl her first piano when she was only three years old.

It was a little pink piano with animal stickers on either side, and each key had a corresponding letter of the alphabet painted just above it. Using the little book that accompanied the piano, Mrs. Houston had helped Victoria to play the songs that were spelled out in the book, until gradually, Victoria could play by herself.

Arriving home, Mrs. Houston parked the car in the driveway and went inside.

Mr. Houston and the two children sat around the kitchen table, and Mrs. Houston knew by the almost audible sound of silence that there was something wrong.

"How did it go?" asked Mr. Houston, as Mrs. Houston took off her coat and put down her car keys.

"Okay," she replied, pulling up a chair, "but what's

wrong with all of you? You look like you are in shock."

"It's the piano, Mom," blurted out Darren, who could barely contain himself. "This time it played for me. I was just practicing my scales..."

Dad frowned in Darren's direction.

"You were what?" he prompted.

"Well, I was about to practice my scales," he corrected. "I was trying to hold down as many black notes as I could with one hand and making my feet reach the pedals at the same time when it started again!"

"What did?" asked Mrs. Houston.

Mr. Houston cleared his throat.

"The piano started playing itself again, Emily. Just like before, repeating the notes over and over."

"The same song?" asked Mrs. Houston.

"No, not this time," replied Mr. Houston. Trying to smile, he said, "I think it's trying to show us it has more than one song in its repertoire."

Mrs. Houston glanced at Victoria.

"Are you all right?" she asked, reaching for her daughter's hand.

"Yes, I'm all right, Mom, thanks. I was scared before when I thought it was only me that caused the piano to play, but today it was Darren who was playing when the piano completely took control. I'm really curious now, though. I'd love to know what's really going on."

Mrs. Houston took the program from her purse and placed it on the kitchen table.

"Okay," she said, "here's the story so far." And she told them what she knew about Nurse Jessica Perry.

"I remember her, of course, I do," said Mr. Houston. "But what does all this mean? Do you think it was her piano that we bought? A haunted piano that only plays her music?"

Looking at her young son's face, eyes widening at every word his father said, Mrs. Houston shook her head in Mr. Houston's direction.

"Of course not," she said. "I mean, you have to be dead before you can haunt things or people, don't you? And as far as I know, Jessica's alive and well and living a few hundred miles away."

Almost to herself, she added quietly, "But it would explain why I haven't received a card or a letter from her in years."

Then, realizing all eyes were on her, she shook herself and gave a little laugh.

"Oh come on you guys, don't look so serious. I don't mean to scare you. It probably has nothing to do with Nurse Perry at all."

"We're not scared, Mom," said Darren, bravely. Though in all honesty, words like "dead" and "haunted" were two of his least favorites. He wondered if he could sleep in Victoria's room that night without her knowing.

"Right," said Mr. Houston, getting up to open the oven door. "Dinner should be almost... Oh no!"

"What is it?" asked Mrs. Houston, turning

toward her husband.

"I am afraid the meatloaf you asked me to cook is a bit, err, overdone."

The meatloaf he removed from the oven was black and barely recognizable.

"But I wrote down 'cook for one hour at 350°F,'" said Mrs. Houston.

"Oh, that was a 3?" He put the burnt offering in the trash can before adding, "I thought it said 450."

Opening the kitchen drawer, Mrs. Houston pulled out a menu.

"Okay, guys, who wants pizza?"

# CHAPTER SIX

## Milk and Cookies

Squinting at her alarm clock, Victoria saw it was 1 a.m. and wondered what had woken her up. Then she realized she was not alone in the bed.

Darren, she thought, looking at his sleeping face. When did he come in here? And didn't he look angelic when he was asleep.

She closed her eyes, but sleep eluded her. She tossed and turned and plumped up her pillow, but all to no avail. She finally decided she was thirsty and got out of bed. She put on her slippers and robe and crept quietly along the hallway to the stairs.

"Victoria," she heard as she reached the second stair. She froze.

Surely the piano can't talk, she thought. Her heart pounded in her chest. Then, slowly lifting her slippered foot to continue her descent, she heard the voice again.

"Victoria!"

This time, though, she recognized the voice as her brother's, and she turned to see him peering at her in the dark.

"Shh," she put her fingers to her lips, then extended her hand upward and motioned for him to come toward her.

The two children crept quietly down the stairs hand in hand and made their way into the kitchen.

Seated at the table with glasses of milk and plates of cookies, the children kept their voices low as they spoke.

"Can't we turn on the light?" Darren asked his sister.

"No," she replied. "We don't want to wake Mom and Dad. The moon's really bright tonight, anyway.

We don't need the light on."

"Why and when did you come into my room?" asked Victoria. "And stop doing that!"

Darren stopped picking the chocolate chips out of his cookie and took a large gulp of milk.

"No reason," he lied. "I was just a little cold, that's all."

"Cold?" said Victoria scornfully. "In the middle of one of the warmest springs we've ever known, you were cold? Tell the truth, Darren. You were afraid, weren't you?"

"Afraid? Afraid of what?" he stammered. "I'm not afraid, Victoria. I told you, I was just cold."

"All right, Darren," his sister relented, reminding herself that he was only six years old and that she herself had been scared the first time the piano had played.

"Look, if I admit to being just a teensy bit scared, you can admit to it too. I promise I won't tell Simon. Anyway, bet you if this happened in his house, he'd be blubbering like a baby."

The thought of Simon, his best friend, who always had to play the part of the hero no matter what game they played, blubbering like a baby cheered Darren up.

As quickly as he had smiled, though, a worried frown spread across his face.

"Victoria," he began.

"Yeah?"

"Would you think I was being really silly if I suggested something about the piano?"

"No, of course I wouldn't." Victoria looked up from her empty plate. "What is it?"

"Well," Darren began slowly, "you know this Nurse Perry person Mom was talking about, and how the piano keeps playing her songs?"

"Well, we know one of the songs is hers, yes," agreed Victoria.

"Well, do you think it's possible...that maybe..."

"Darren, spit it out!" His sister began to lose

patience. "Come on, I want to go back to bed, so hurry up and say what you're thinking."

"Promise you won't laugh?"

Sighing, Victoria lifted her glass and plate from the table and walked toward the sink.

"I'm going to bed," she said.

"Okay, okay, I'll say it," said Darren.

His sister sat back down.

"I think someone murdered Nurse Perry, put her body inside the piano, and her spirit is playing the songs to let us know her body is in there," he said.

Victoria looked aghast.

"Murdered? Put her body inside the piano? No wonder you couldn't sleep, Darren. That sounds horrible!"

"I knew you wouldn't believe me," her brother sighed.

"Well, let's face it, Darren," she said, a little more gently this time, "it is a little far-fetched. But then again, if you were to tell someone about a piano that played by itself, they would think that was far-fetched, wouldn't they?"

The two children sat quietly for a while.

"Do you want to go and look?" ventured Victoria.

Darren said nothing for a while, then said, "I think we have to. I don't see how anyone can sleep in this house when there might be a dead body inside our piano!"

# CHAPTER SEVEN

## Just Checking

The house was deathly silent as brother and sister crept along the hall. Just before they reached the playroom, Victoria stepped on something sharp and had to stop herself from crying out.

"What's wrong?" asked Darren.

His sister bent down and picked up a plastic dinosaur.

"That's what's wrong," she hissed at him. "When are you going to learn to pick up your toys?"

Shaking her head, she tucked the dinosaur under her arm, intending to throw it into one of the boxes in the playroom.

The two children entered the room.

"Did you bring Dad's flashlight?" asked Darren. Victoria nodded and held up the flashlight in her left hand. They crept to the far end of the room where the piano stood.

"Okay," said Victoria, "we're not going to be able to see anything unless we stand on top of the stool."

Pulling it toward her, trying to make as little noise as possible, she motioned to Darren to climb up.

"We'll both have to stand on it, then one of us can lift the lid and the other one can shine the flashlight so we can see inside," she said.

Darren moved toward the stool to do as his sister said. He really wished he'd kept his big mouth shut. He was afraid now. The playroom looked very different in the moonlight. Every toy looked sinister, and he had jumped at the sight of a huge shadow reflected on the wall. Looking down, he realized it was one of his action figures, the one that had a yellow and green skull instead of a face and bright red glowing coals where there should have been eyes. Funny how it looked so menacing when magnified to six times its normal size!

His heart pounding, he stepped on top of the stool. Suddenly, there was a tapping noise at the window.

"What was that?" He grabbed his sister, almost knocking both himself and her off their unsteady perch.

"It's only the wind," she whispered, turning toward the window. He saw that the window was open and that the curtain blew, causing the Venetian blinds to rattle against the windowpane. He steadied himself again and took the flashlight his sister held out toward him.

"Ready?" she asked.

He nodded uncertainly. What if there is a body in there, he thought. What then?

Victoria leaned forward and began to lift the lid. This time the tapping noise was louder. Only now it was more of a scuffling noise.

She glanced back at her brother.

"Did you hear that?" she whispered.

Did he hear it? He was petrified! It hadn't been the wind at all! It was the body inside the piano. He knew it was! It scratching helplessly at its wooden grave, trying to get out! He'd known it all along!

In his rush to get down from the stool, he dropped the flashlight and, trying to catch it before it hit the ground, completely lost his balance and grabbed onto his sister's leg trying to save himself. Victoria tried to hold onto the piano to stop herself from falling, but the partially lifted lid slammed shut on her fingers, causing her to emit a bloodcurdling scream.

Minutes later, Mr. Houston threw open the playroom door and switched on the light. He could not believe the sight that greeted him.

Victoria, tears sliding down her face, knelt on the floor nursing her rapidly swelling fingers. Her brother, meanwhile, was not far from her with his leg twisted uncomfortably beneath him.

"What on earth is going on?" he asked, aware that he seemed to have been asking that question a lot lately.

Victoria tried to speak, sobs choking her.

"Oh Dad, we're sorry, we were just trying to see inside the piano. We didn't want to wake you up! My fingers," she wept. "I think they're broken!"

Mrs. Houston had by now joined them in the playroom and was helping Darren to sit up.

"Are you all right? Do you think you can stand?" she asked her son, who was also in tears.

"I've probably broken my leg in five places!" he wailed.

"It's okay," his mother said. "Hold my hands and try to stand. There you go."

Tentatively, and clinging tightly to his mom, the young boy moved to a standing position.

"Ow, it hurts, Mom. It really hurts!"

"Okay, dear, I know, but just hold onto me and try taking a couple of steps."

Mrs. Houston could tell that although Darren had undoubtedly hurt himself, his leg was not broken. Thank goodness for that, she thought.

Mr. Houston, meanwhile, was shaking his head as he looked at his daughter's fingers.

"Victoria, Victoria, what are we going do with you?" He held her hands gently. "Come on, stop crying and tell me what this was all about."

Through muffled sobs, Victoria told the story to her father who sat in disbelief.

"And then there was a scuffling noise, and Darren dropped the flashlight and..."

She stopped and turned toward the piano.

"Listen, there it is again."

The whole family listened. And, sure enough, a strange noise did seem to come from the piano. Darren moved closer to his mom, involuntarily tightening his grip on her fingers.

"See," he almost accused his sister. "I told you it wasn't the wind. There is something inside the piano!"

As Mr. Houston stood up and went to take a closer look, the sound came again, but this time from behind the piano rather than in it.

"Give me a hand, honey," he said to his wife, and the two of them pushed one end of the piano out from the wall.

"There's your dead body." He grinned.

A little sparrow was curled up in the corner of the room.

"It's only a baby," said Mrs. Houston. "There's a nest of them outside our bedroom window. It must have flown in through this open window and the poor little thing wasn't able to find its way back out."

Sore leg almost completely forgotten, Darren joined his parents looking at the poor little bird.

"Is it hurt?" he asked.

"I don't think so, son," replied his dad. "Just a bit

shaken and probably more than a little scared. I'll try and pick him up so he can get back to the nest."

The little bird, not yet having the sense to know he could simply flap his wings and fly off, hopped around the floor in fear when he saw the huge giant approach him. Mr. Houston eventually managed to lift the little bird and after checking there was nothing wrong with it, set it outside on the window ledge.

"There, he'll be just fine now. He'll go right back to his family."

He turned back to see Mrs. Houston gently rubbing Victoria's fingers.

"Dead bodies, you say," she chastised her. "And you have your big recital next week too—thank goodness your fingers aren't broken—we'll just have to hope the swelling goes down quickly."

Victoria sighed and nodded her head in agreement.

"It was pretty silly, I guess. I mean we could

have waited until morning," she said looking at her brother, who was examining his leg for bruises, cuts, and anything else he could brag about to Simon.

"I don't know if I'll be able to go to school tomorrow," he announced.

"Yes, well, we'll see about that in the morning." Mrs. Houston smiled, relieved that no one seemed to have suffered more than surface bruising and injured pride. Hugging both her children, she turned them in the direction of the door and sent them upstairs to bed. "Go on, now, off to bed, or we'll all oversleep tomorrow."

"All right, Mom, Dad, good night," they chorused and walked wearily upstairs.

"What a night!" Mrs. Houston turned to her husband. "Dead bodies in pianos, I mean it's just too ridiculous for words." She yawned sleepily. "Come on, let's go to bed, I'm exhausted."

Mr. Houston nodded. "Yes, I'm right behind you."

Mrs. Houston left the room, but as soon as she put her foot on the third stair, she realized her husband wasn't following. She went back downstairs and pushed open the playroom door.

"Roger..." she began, then stopped as she realized her husband was shining the flashlight inside the piano.

Looking up, he grinned sheepishly.

"Just checking," he said.

# CHAPTER EIGHT

## Some News

The next morning, everyone sat sleepily around the breakfast table.

"I'm so tired," said Victoria. "I must have only slept four hours last night."

"I know, dear." Her mother smiled. "We all feel the same way. We can have an early night tonight after we get back from Treetops."

"What's Treetops?" asked Darren, looking curiously at his mom.

"It's a house your father and I have been looking at, and we'd like you both to come see it before we decide on anything."

"Decide what?" asked Victoria, looking from one

parent to the other.

"Whether to buy it or not," said Mr. Houston. "It's a beautiful house. I know you're both going to like it. We're very lucky to be given the opportunity to buy it."

Victoria stopped eating.

"Buy another house? What? Leave our home? Why? When? I don't want to leave here. Mom?" She turned toward her mother. "Do you want to do this too?" she asked. "I thought you loved it here."

Mrs. Houston looked at her husband anxiously then back toward Victoria.

"It is a lovely house, sweetheart," she said reassuringly, "and the yard is huge—wait until you see it!"

Victoria pushed her plate away from her. "I don't want to move," she said. "I want to stay here."

Darren reached over to his sister's plate. "Aren't you going to eat your bacon?" he asked, already lifting the food to his mouth.

Victoria looked at him with disgust. "You're so gross sometimes," she said. "Don't you even care about what they're saying?"

"Of course I care," he said. "It's just that I'm...Hey, what did you do that for?" He turned angrily toward Victoria, who had clamped her hand over his mouth and was staring wide-eyed at the kitchen door.

"Shh," she told him. "Be quiet—listen."

Everyone was still and could hear the sound of the piano playing loudly and angrily.

"Not again!" Mr. Houston shook his head and jumped to his feet.

Mrs. Houston and the two children followed and made their way to the playroom. Mr. Houston opened the door, and the family watched the piano and listened to the now familiar song.

The piano thumped and banged, the vibrations causing the instrument to move slightly along the floor. The children stayed close to their parents, afraid of the angry sounds and air of tension that

63

filled the room. Eventually, the piano seemed to tire and began to play quieter, and the children became less afraid.

"Will you be all right in the house by yourself?" asked Mr. Houston.

"Of course I will," replied Mrs. Houston. "Don't worry about me. You go to work, and I'll drop the children off at school. I'll be just fine. What could the piano possibly do to me?"

"If you're sure. It's just that everything's so weird right now." He looked at his watch. "I really have to go, but I'll pick you all up at six tonight, and we can drive over to Treetops."

As though reacting to some sort of signal, the piano once more burst into angry banging and thumping, almost as though at the mention of the name of the new house.

"Wow!" said Darren. "It's getting mad again!"

Mr. Houston pulled the door shut and led his family away from the noise. As they went back into the kitchen, Mrs. Houston looked thoughtful.

"I'm going to call Jessica today," she said. "I don't know if she'll be of any help or not, but it's worth a try, right?"

"But you have no idea where she lives," said her husband.

"No," she replied, "but I do know where she works. I'll call the hospital."

# CHAPTER NINE

## Treetops

When Mr. Houston arrived home that night just after six, Mrs. Houston and the two children were waiting. They got into the car, Victoria looking unhappy, and drove off in the direction of the large house.

"How was your day?" Mrs. Houston asked Mr. Houston distractedly.

"Fine," he replied. "How was yours? Any luck contacting Jessica?"

His wife sighed. She might upset the children, she thought, but they knew so much already that there was no point in trying to hide anything from them.

"I called the hospital this morning," she said, "and asked if I could speak to Nurse Jessica Perry. The young girl asked who I was then put me through to the head nurse. She's dead, Roger. Jessica's dead!"

Mrs. Houston bit her lip and looked down at her hands. "She died over eight years ago, not long after she moved, apparently. I feel so awful, you know, no wonder I didn't hear from her—poor Jessica."

Arriving at the foot of the hill that would take the family on up to Treetops, Mr. Houston parked the car and turned off the engine.

"What happened?" he asked his wife quietly.

"A car accident," she said slowly. "A freak car accident. A semi truck lost control and ran into her car. She was killed instantly. Apparently she didn't suffer, so I guess that's a blessing."

Her husband shook his head. "That's awful, Emily. I'm so sorry."

"I know, such a tragedy," she agreed. "She was on her way to her publisher, according to what the head nurse said. She'd confided her musical ambitions to her the day before. Seemingly she had just completed a new piece of music and was taking it to her publisher on her day off to see what he thought of it. So I called him, too.

"The head nurse could only remember part of the firm's name, but I found them online. I said I'd recently heard 'The Ancient Oak' and wondered if Jessica Perry had written anything else. He was very helpful and was able to tell me she'd had one other piece of work published, 'La Niña Hermosa.' Apparently it's Spanish for 'the beautiful girl.' Her mother was from Mexico."

She paused for a moment, glancing in the mirror at her two children. Both were listening intently, waiting to hear what she would say next. She cleared her throat.

"So, anyway, I asked them to send copies of the two pieces of music to me. I think I'm pretty sure by now the one the piano plays most often and most angrily is 'The Ancient Oak,' and I'd say it's a fair bet that 'La Niña Hermosa' is the other one. Anyway, let's just wait and see, okay?"

She forced a smile. "Now come on, you two, don't look so glum. We'll get to the bottom of this mystery soon, and life will go back to being dull and boring again!"

Darren had unconsciously moved closer to his sister in the back seat and was now holding her hand.

"Ow, Darren, not so tight," she yelped. "My fingers are still tender from the piano slamming incident—which also happened to be your fault!"

Darren removed his hand indignantly.

"Sorry," he mumbled, "I forgot."

Mr. Houston turned the key in the ignition and moved away from the side of the road.

"Let's just wait until the music sheets arrive and we'll see if they are one and the same, then we can take it from there."

A few minutes later, they arrived outside the

house. The old gentleman, seated in his sun room as usual, raised his hand in greeting. Darren slammed the car door shut and gazed in wonder.

"The yard's enormous, Dad. We can play football and baseball. Simon would never find me here in a game of hide-and-seek. Wow! When are we moving in?"

Victoria looked at him.

"Traitor," she said. "Have you no loyalty to your home? Are you so flippant that you'd just move so you could play hide-and-seek?" She huffed and folded her arms across her chest.

Mrs. Houston put her hand gently on her daughter's shoulders.

"Come on, everyone, let's go inside. And don't be so hard on your brother, Victoria. He is only six, remember?"

Mrs. Houston and Victoria walked in the direction of the front door with Mr. Houston following closely behind.

"Daaaad," shouted Darren, running to keep up. "What does flippant mean?"

Even Victoria, sulking and upset, had to admit the house was beautiful.

The old gentleman was charming and had instructed the family to feel free to explore every room. Though he was obviously unable to accompany them, he told them to remember any questions and he'd answer them later.

Over coffee and cake, served by the old man's daughter, he talked fondly of his home and knowledgeably of its history. Though she had been determined not to, Victoria felt herself drawn to old Mr. Lawrence and to his house.

Darren was reaching out for his fourth slice of cake when a look from his father caused him to withdraw his hand and sit back in his seat.

"So," began Mrs. Williams, Mr. Lawrence's daughter, "what do you think?"

"We're very impressed," answered Mrs. Houston.

"It's a beautiful house. You must have loved living here as a child."

"Yes, indeed." Mrs. Williams smiled. "I have lots of happy memories, I have to say, but you can't live in the past forever. There comes a time when you simply have to move on, isn't that right, Dad?"

Mr. Lawrence turned back from the window to look at his daughter. His wife had died almost ten years ago now, and he knew he couldn't realistically expect to stay in this house for much longer.

Elizabeth, his daughter, had been very good to him over the years, and he knew it made sense for him to go and live with her and her husband in their modern house in town.

"Yes, dear, you're right, we all have to move on at some time in our lives." He hastily wiped away a tear before anyone could see it and managed a little smile. He liked this family, and he didn't mind the thought of them living in his precious home. It'll bring the place to life again, he thought, the sound of children running through the house.

Adjusting the blanket tucked over his legs, he leaned forward in his wheelchair. "Now then, young man." He held out the plate toward Darren. "What about that fourth slice of cake?"

𝄢          𝄢          𝄢

Darren and Victoria sat on the wooden bench outside the house while Mr. and Mrs. Houston said their goodbyes.

"We still have to put our own house on the market, you understand," Mr. Houston was saying. "But we are very interested in this one."

Mr. Lawrence and his daughter nodded.

"I'd be very happy to see you and your family living here," the old man said. "I know when to accept gracious defeat." He smiled at his daughter, who reached for his hand.

"It was lovely to meet you all," she said to the family. "We hope to hear from you soon."

"We'll be in touch," said Mr. Houston, "and we

do understand that if another buyer comes along you'll sell to them. After all, you can't wait for us forever!"

"I have a feeling we'll be doing business, young man," said Mr. Lawrence, as he turned his wheelchair and went back inside.

Victoria and Darren got up to join their parents on the driveway. They waved to Mr. Lawrence, who was by now back in the sun room, and Darren stopped and bent to pick up some acorns. Looking up, he had to shade his eyes from the sun.

"What an enormous tree," he observed looking at the huge oak that stood to the left of the conservatory.

"Yeah," his sister agreed, "must have been here for centuries! Come on, let's get into the car. Mom and Dad are waiting."

# CHAPTER TEN

## You've Got Mail

The swelling had disappeared on Victoria's fingers after a couple of days and she resumed her position on the stool practicing the piano.

The music her mom had asked to be sent from the publisher did not arrive until three days later, during which time the piano burst to life on more than a few occasions.

Sometimes it played gently, almost soothingly, but other times the whole playroom seemed to shake with its anger.

Strangely, the morning the man called from the estate agency to take photographs of the house was one of the days the piano played at its loudest and most violent. When he began to hammer the for sale sign into the yard, the noise from the piano was almost deafening.

"My daughter's practicing for a recital," Mr. Houston mumbled apologetically to the man. "A little heavy-handed, I'm afraid."

The man looked at him oddly, or was it Mr. Houston's imagination, and left soon after.

Of course, as soon as his car disappeared from sight, the furious playing stopped.

Though perhaps uneasily, the family became used to the music filling the house and tried not to let it disrupt their lives too much.

Mrs. Houston was the first one downstairs each morning, checking the mail because she truly felt somehow that the clue to what this was all about was contained in those music sheets.

When finally the large brown envelope was pushed through the mailbox, Mrs. Houston was almost afraid to open it. Victoria spotted it propped against the toaster when she came downstairs for breakfast.

"Is that it, Mom, is that the music?" she asked.

"I think so. I feel a bit uneasy about opening it."

"Then I'll do it," said her daughter. Victoria tore open the envelope and looked at the enclosed papers. "It's them, all right, Mom. 'The Ancient Oak' and 'La Niña Hermosa.'"

Victoria stared hard at "The Ancient Oak."

"It's definitely the same song," she told her mother as she read the notes. "I've heard it so many times now I think I could write the notes down myself."

"Come on, Mom, let's go into the playroom. I want to try playing these for myself."

The two made their way to the playroom.

Victoria took her place on the stool. Almost afraid, without really knowing why, Mrs. Houston stood beside her daughter and watched her play.

Victoria played as though she herself had written

both songs. She didn't hesitate at all. She played with a comfortable familiarity, which gave the music a delightful flow. When she finished, she turned toward her mother and gave a sad smile. Her eyes had filled with tears.

"She must have been a beautiful person, Mom, to be able to write such beautiful music."

Her mother smiled in agreement just as the door creaked open and Mr. Houston and Darren stepped inside.

"We weren't sure if it was the piano or you," said Mr. Houston wryly. "Then when neither of you were in the kitchen, we realized it must be you."

Seeing his daughter's tear-filled eyes, he looked questioningly at his wife.

"Jessica's music arrived, I guess?" he asked.

"Yes, this morning. It's very beautiful, if you just remember to play it at the right tempo! Come on Victoria, let's leave the music for now." She gently pulled her daughter to her feet. "Go and take a shower, dear, and get ready for school. We can look at the music again later."

Victoria left the room, followed by her parents.

"Come on, Darren, you too," said Mr. Houston.

"Coming," replied Darren. "I just found a toy I lost months ago."

As he walked past the piano toward the toy box, he could see that the keys of the piano shone and glistened more than usual. Curious, he picked up his toy and went to look at the piano more closely. He touched the keys tentatively and was amazed to find that his fingers came away wet!

Jumping back, he decided to get out of the room fast. As he closed the door behind him, he shrugged. If I didn't know any better, he thought, I'd swear the piano had been crying!

# CHAPTER ELEVEN

## A Storm is Brewing

"Victoria, where are you?" shouted Mrs. Houston from the hallway.

"Up here, Mom," her daughter replied. "I'm in my bedroom."

Victoria then appeared at the top of the stairs and hung her head over the banister.

"Come down a minute. I'm going out, and I need to talk to you first."

Victoria came downstairs and followed her mother onto the front porch.

"I'm going to the store. Are you sure you don't want to come?"

Her daughter shook her head.

"Neither does Darren," said Mrs. Houston. "Okay, then, what time is it now?" She checked her watch. "Six o'clock. I'll go now and I should be back in an hour and a half. Dad has to stay late for a meeting, but he should be home around the same time as me. Okay? Darren's playing with Simon outside—I'll tell him not to go too far and to do what you tell him."

Victoria raised her eyebrows realizing it was a futile request.

"Now, where are my car keys?"

Mrs. Houston's car had no sooner left the driveway than the phone rang. Victoria answered. It was her father.

"Victoria, hi, let me speak to your mom, please?"

"You just missed her, Dad. She just left for the grocery store."

"She did?" There was silence for a moment. "Look, Victoria, it seems like this meeting may go on longer than I thought it would, so I may not get home until closer to 8:30 p.m."

"Okay, Dad, I'll let Mom know when she gets back."

"Thanks, sorry about this. Will you guys be okay?"

"Of course we will." She took another sip of the soda she had taken from the fridge. "Mom will be home in just over an hour. Don't worry, Dad, we'll be just fine."

After saying goodbye to her father, Victoria put the phone down and went into the front room. She looked out of the window to see Darren was still playing in the yard, then glanced up to check if the window was open. The temperature both inside and out of the house was unbelievable for this time of year. The window was open, as were all the other windows in the house, but there still didn't seem to be any air.

Finishing what was left of her drink, Victoria went back upstairs to finish her homework.

"Now, do we need breakfast cereal or not?" Mrs. Houston mumbled to herself in the store. She picked up a box anyway and made her way to the checkout.

"It got awfully dark outside," said one of the women in the line. "It's practically an eclipse."

Mrs. Houston looked at the cashier. The young girl continued to scan the goods coming toward her on the conveyor belt and nodded her head distractedly.

Mrs. Houston then looked at the sky and was shocked to see how dark it had become since she had entered the store.

She checked her watch. She had only been gone about an hour. She hoped Darren had gone inside the house, because she was now afraid that maybe a storm was brewing. There was certainly something in the air. She'd be home soon, anyway, it was her turn next.

The woman in front pulled out her card, almost

at the same time as the bored checkout girl's help sign came on.

Mrs. Houston sighed. Why do I always get in the wrong line, and why is it always when I'm in a rush?

# CHAPTER TWELVE

## Gone Dark

Darren had come inside—not because of the storm—but because Simon had been called inside by his mother and he was bored playing outside in the yard by himself.

He walked upstairs to his sister's room and entered without knocking.

"How many times have I told you to knock?" she said, not moving from her position on the bed. She was lying face down, reading a textbook and listening to music.

"Sorry," mumbled Darren, though he wasn't. He couldn't care less who came into his bedroom and certainly would never think of asking anyone to knock before entering.

"I'm hungry," he told his sister.

"So, what else is new?" she asked, still not lifting her head. "Why don't you go and get a bag of chips?"

"There aren't any," he replied. "I hope Mom brings some back from the store."

"Actually," said Victoria, putting down her book, "I'm hungry too. Let's go see what we can put in the microwave!"

Downstairs in the kitchen, Victoria turned on the light.

"I can't believe it's so dark so early," she said.

She looked out of the window at the sky. "I hope there isn't going to be a thunderstorm."

Darren emerged from the depths of the freezer, a package in each hand.

"What do you want?" he asked. "Pizza rolls or chicken nuggets?"

"I don't care." His sister, who was helping herself to more soda, shrugged. Really, it was so hot, there probably was about to be a thunderstorm, she thought.

"Then we'll have both," said Darren happily. "Here."

He handed her the boxes and Victoria read the instructions quickly and put the pizza rolls in the oven and the chicken nuggets in the microwave.

The first crack of thunder took them both completely by surprise. Victoria was seated on top of one of the tall kitchen stools leaning against the breakfast bar, while Darren stood beside the microwave, counting down the minutes as though he didn't trust the oven to do it on its own. Darren turned quickly to face his sister.

"Ughhh," she whispered. "Please not a thunderstorm."

The next crack sent her flying off the stool and away from the window to stand beside her brother.

"It's okay, Victoria. It's only a little storm. We'll be fine."

Victoria was, and always had been, terrified of thunder and lightning. She had spent many nights in her parents' bed when storms had raged before. Darren, on the other hand, was totally unafraid and loved to stand at the window watching the bolts of lightning flash across the sky.

Darren turned his attention back to the microwave to see how much cooking time remained when there was a huge clap of thunder and the house was plunged into darkness.

"Victoria!" Darren shouted.

He reached for his sister's arm, missing completely and instead knocking the can of soda from her hand, causing it to hit the floor and let its contents spill out. His sister's face was illuminated by the lightning, which streaked across the sky, and the whole kitchen was lit up, but only for an instant. Victoria grabbed her brother's hand.

"It's all right, Darren." She tried to sound reassuring, but her voice was far from steady as she continued. "Mom and Dad will be here soon. All we have to do is stay calm and before we know it, the power will be back on."

"A power outage? Does that mean I can't have my chicken nuggets?" he asked. "I'm starving."

Not letting go of his hand, Victoria felt her way to the pantry and took a huge bar of chocolate from inside.

"Here," she offered the bar to her brother. "That should keep you going for a while."

Their eyes grew accustomed to the dark and the two now looked at one another.

"Should we stay here, do you think?" asked Darren. "Or should we go upstairs?"

Victoria was about to answer when she heard a loud slam from the front of the house.

"What was that?" She looked at Darren.

"It's probably Mom!" he said excitedly.

Before he could shout for his mom, Victoria put her hand over his mouth.

"Shh," she whispered urgently. "How do you know it's Mom—I didn't hear a car pulling up, did you?"

Pulling her hand away from his mouth, Darren turned on her angrily.

"How do you expect to hear anything above the noise of the thunder?" he asked. "Of course it's Mom. Who else would it be?"

"Come over here, Darren," she instructed. "Come with me. We'll get Dad's flashlight, then we'll go investigate."

After considerable fumbling in the drawer, Victoria triumphantly produced the flashlight and the two children left the kitchen hand in hand.

It wasn't necessary to try to be quiet going along the hall, because the sound of the storm raged furiously all around them. At this point, both children knew that it was not their mother who had come in through the front door. They would have run into her in the hall by now.

Wanting desperately to stop and change direction to go back to the safety of the kitchen, Victoria knew that she had to make sure the front door was firmly locked first. Tightening her grip on Darren's hand, she continued to shine the flashlight in front of them, placing one foot in front of the other, until they reached the door of the front porch.

"I'm scared, Victoria," said Darren, his voice almost inaudible over the sound of the storm. "I want Mom and Dad to come home."

Victoria bent down closer to her brother. "I'm scared too," she said, "but we have to lock the front door, then we can go call Dad at the office and tell him what's going on. He'll be home in fifteen minutes, max, I promise. In fact, he'll probably meet Mom outside in the driveway!"

Victoria sounded a lot braver than she felt and wished more than anything else in the world that her parents were here with them now. As she straightened up from talking to Darren, the door slammed again, only this time there was the added noise of something smashing on the floor. Victoria swallowed hard and started to walk forward.

It was at that moment that the flashlight batteries went out.

# CHAPTER THIRTEEN

## The Piano Beckons

Plunged once again into complete darkness, the children fell into each other's arms and clung together. Victoria sank down onto the floor, pulling her brother with her.

Darren was crying now, and Victoria was trying not to. As they sat there, the door repeatedly slammed open and shut, open and shut, thunder cracked and lightning flashed, and again there was the added sound of something breaking and smashing onto the floor.

"I don't want to go any farther, Victoria, please. There must be someone on the porch, right?" He looked up at his sister.

"I don't know if there's anyone there, Darren, but I don't feel like going much farther myself, especially without the flashlight."

The thunder had quieted to a rumble for now, and the children became aware of another noise. They listened intently.

"The piano!" said Victoria. "It's calling to us," she said, getting to her feet. "Come on," she told Darren, "let's go to the playroom—the sound of the piano will guide us through the darkness and we can use the phone in there to call Dad."

The frightened little boy got to his feet, clinging to his sister the whole time. He didn't bother to question her instructions; he just wanted this whole nightmare to be over.

Holding on to the wall, and to each other, the children returned along the route they had just come, all the while aware of the slamming of the front door interspersed with loud cracks of thunder. At the same time, the piano could be heard playing, as though it was beckoning to them to come to the playroom.

An extra loud bang of thunder was followed by a flash of lightning that momentarily lit up the house.

"Aargh!" wailed Darren loudly, almost causing his sister to jump out of her skin.

"What now?" she asked, turning back to him.

"There." He pointed to a picture on the wall.

Victoria squinted in the darkness. "It's the picture of you and me that Mom likes so much," she said. "What's so scary?"

"Phew," he breathed a sigh of relief. "Looked like alien creatures in the dark."

If she hadn't been so frightened, Victoria would have laughed. She thought the picture made them look like alien creatures in the daylight!

They had almost reached the playroom. As soon as they stepped in, Victoria picked up the phone.

"How will you see to dial the number?" asked Darren.

Victoria set the phone down and replied, "No need to worry about that—it's dead. The phone lines must be down too."

They looked across the room, where the piano still played.

"How strong do you feel?" Victoria asked her brother.

"Depends what for." He looked at her curiously.

"I think we should wheel the piano over in front of the door so that no one can get in." Then, seeing his ashen face, she added, "At least until Mom and Dad get home. As soon as we know it's them, we'll let them in—okay?"

Her brother looked doubtfully at the instrument in the corner.

"Do you think we can?" he asked.

"Of course," said Victoria with bravado. "Let's do it!"

And they did. While the storm outside still showed no sign of stopping, the two of them

determinedly pushed and pulled at the piano until they had it positioned right against the playroom door.

"I feel safer now," said Victoria, smiling at her brother. He smiled back, reaching in his pocket for the half-melted chocolate bar.

"Let's sit over there on the sofa and eat this," he said. "We can tell stories for a while."

The piano was quiet now and looked almost to be standing guard over them both. Every now and then, a flash of lightning would light up the room, and the children would use this as an opportunity to retrieve something from the toy boxes. So far, Darren had recovered a wooden bridge, which had once been part of his train set; an unbelievably intact dinosaur jigsaw puzzle; a gel pen; and a multicolored flashlight.

"A flashlight!" exclaimed Victoria, who had discovered her little pink piano from all those years ago and was gently running her fingers over the keys.

"Does it work?" she asked excitedly.

Darren moved the switch from off to on, and the two were delighted to see a green light dance on the wall.

"Perfect," said Victoria, clapping her hands. "Point it up between us so we can both see."

Doing as he was told, Darren wedged the flashlight between the small wooden bridge and an old nursery rhyme book and went off to rummage in what looked like the creepy crawly toy box!

Victoria was still humming "The Ancient Oak" since the piano had played it earlier and was absentmindedly playing the notes on her pink piano. She looked at the keys as she hit each one, the letter D corresponding with the first note she played. The second note read O above it, the third N, then back to O again. When she touched the fifth key, Victoria was beginning to realize this was not just a jumble of letters, instead it looked like the piano was trying to give her a message.

"Darren," she called excitedly. "Darren, come and see this. The song means something—hurry."

Darren scrambled over toward his sister and watched.

"Get a pen! Quickly, write down each letter as I play the notes."

She hummed out loud as she slowly picked out each note.

DONOT

Darren looked at the letters he had written then moved closer to see what the rest of the message would be.

Victoria played the next note and the next, until the message was clear to them both.

DONOTBUYTREETOPS

"Do not buy Treetops!" said Darren. "But why?

It doesn't make sense."

Victoria looked at the large piano standing on the other side of the room and wondered. Was this what it had been trying to tell them ever since it had come into their possession? A message from the grave conveyed through a piano?

What Victoria would have dismissed a few months ago as being utter nonsense, she now wasn't so quick to disregard.

"Victoria," Darren insisted. "Why would the piano tell us not to buy a house? I don't understand."

His sister leaned back against the sofa.

"I don't understand either, Darren. I'm not sure that I ever will, but I'm getting used to not understanding."

The two sat for a moment in silence, then Victoria pointed out, "There hasn't been any thunder or lightning for at least ten minutes. Maybe the storm's moved on."

Sleepily, they cuddled up together, pulling a

blanket over them. To the sound of heavy rainfall outside, they fell sound asleep.

# CHAPTER FOURTEEN

## The Final Song

"The telephone is working again," said Mr. Houston, as he tried the phone for the hundredth time that morning.

"That's good, dear," replied his wife. "Now all we need is for the electricity to come back on and we're in business."

The previous night Mr. and Mrs. Houston had, indeed, met one another outside the house. Mrs. Houston's car had simply refused to start when she was ready to leave the store, and she had to take shelter from the storm for awhile before anyone was able to help her.

Eventually, a young man had kindly looked under

her hood and helped her jump her car. She set off slowly, driving carefully back to her children.

Mr. Houston, meanwhile, leaving late from his meeting, had been shocked to find that the closer he got to home the greater number of houses seemed to have been affected by the storm. Most places were in complete darkness.

Pulling onto the road almost at the same time, both jumped from their cars and ran into the gloomy house. They had eventually, after deducing where the children must be, hammered and banged on the door of the playroom until they managed to wake them.

Lots of hugging ensued, followed by Victoria showing her parents, by flashlight, the message she had uncovered earlier.

Astounded, Mr. and Mrs. Houston had made her repeat the song slowly.

"She's right, you know," said Mr. Houston. "That's exactly what it says."

Mrs. Houston nodded. "But why would Jessica not want us to buy another house?" she wondered aloud.

The four spent the night together in Mr. and Mrs. Houston's bedroom, crammed together but safe and happy.

The next morning, Mr. Houston repaired the front door. It had broken one of its hinges the previous night and shattered two of Mrs. Houston's potted plants.

Helping his dad to clean up, Darren couldn't imagine what he and Victoria had been so afraid of last night. A door slamming and a porch full of geraniums and daffodils! So what! He'd tell Simon a very different version of the story, that was for sure!

Victoria and Mrs. Houston were upstairs.

"I'm sure Jessica wrote 'La Niña Hermosa' for you," Mrs. Houston was saying. "She adored you, Victoria, especially since she never had any children of her own."

"Emily," Mr. Houston shouted. "Come down quickly, there's something I have to show you."

Mrs. Houston and Victoria quickly descended the stairs to see what all the fuss was about.

Mr. Houston held out the morning newspaper toward his wife. She glanced at the page. Most articles were concerned with the new mayor, but her husband pointed toward a small feature on the bottom left-hand corner.

## FREAK STORM TRAGEDY

A freak thunderstorm wreaked havoc on the little town of Plessington last night. A large part of the neighborhood lost electricity and phone lines were also affected. Tragically, Mr. Jeremy Lawrence, owner of Treetops on Mill Road, was killed when the large oak tree that stood beside his house was struck by lightning. The tree crashed through the sun room, killing the man instantly. Mr. Lawrence, whose family had lived in Treetops for generations...

Mrs. Houston put the newspaper down on the hall table and leaned against her husband to steady herself. Victoria grabbed the paper and began reading.

"Oh no," she gasped. "Poor old Mr. Lawrence. But don't you see? Mom? Dad? That's why Jessica was warning us not to go. She knew the accident was going to happen. It could have been us who were killed!"

Darren was pulling at his mother's skirt.

"What is it, dear?" she asked distractedly.

"This just came for you," he said, handing her a large brown envelope.

"What? Oh, right, thank you."

Carelessly, she tore it open, her thoughts still with Mr. Lawrence. As she pulled the letter from the envelope, she saw it was from the same publisher who had sent her the two pieces of music Jessica had written.

Dear Mrs. Houston,

Your recent inquiry concerning Miss Jessica Perry caused us to search through files we had previously archived. Miss Perry's file contained a document addressed to a Miss Victoria Houston, however gave no address. In the hopes that it may belong to your family, we are forwarding it to you.

Yours,
Harmony Publishing

Mrs. Houston reached back inside the large envelope and pulled out a slimmer one with Victoria's name on it. She handed it to her daughter.

"From Jessica," she said.

Victoria carefully opened the envelope and removed a sheet of music entitled "La Guardián Angel."

Read on to enjoy an excerpt from another
haunting title in the Creepers series:

# The Gravedigger

by Edgar J. Hyde

Illustrations by Chloe Tyler

# CHAPTER ONE

## The New House

With every crack of lightning, Jamie's shadow was thrown against the wall. Lightning lit up his room for a split second before it was covered again with a blanket of darkness.

Outside, the icy night wind swirled around the graveyard, whistling through the gravestones and running down the old dirt track past the trees to the house at the bottom of the hill.

Inside, the house was in total darkness. The storm had knocked out the power a couple of hours ago, leaving Jamie, his younger sister, Paula, and his father, Andrew, fumbling around their new house in the pitch black, falling over unopened boxes and as usual in these circumstances, trying to scare the living daylights out of each other.

Jamie stood at the bottom of the long spiraling staircase that led upstairs to their bedrooms. He could hear someone moving around, squeaking the bare floorboards in his father's room.

It must be Dad, he thought. Paula's too light to make that kind of noise.

Slowly, he began to climb the stairs looking for Paula. He had an idea where his dad was, but Paula could be hiding anywhere waiting to pounce.

By now, the storm outside was getting worse. As Jamie crept past the window on the landing, another bolt of lightning lit up the staircase and the tall, dark figure that was creeping up the stairs behind him. Jamie continued to make his way up the stairs, completely unaware of the ghostly intruder. As he reached the top, he paused for a second, peering cautiously around the corner.

The door to his father's room was ajar but not

enough for Jamie to see inside. Knowing his family like he did, he knew that someone inside the room was waiting to jump out screaming and yelling.

Then Jamie heard breathing behind him. Quick as a flash he turned to see, but there was only darkness. The tall, dark figure that had floated behind him on the stairs was gone. The whole house was silent—eerily silent.

The creak of the bathroom door shattered the silence, and in a second, Jamie dashed into his little sister's room, leaving the door open a little so that he could still see out.

Then he saw it. The tall figure that followed him from downstairs passed through the bathroom door, turned, and made its way along the hall toward him.

It was a very tall man dressed in a long black cloak with swept back hair and bright white teeth that shone in the moonlight whenever he passed a window.

Before he reached his father's room, the door

opened and a familiar face stepped out from behind it. It was Paula.

The dark man glided along the hallway toward her. Paula, oblivious to what was over her shoulder, slipped out of the room and tiptoed her way down the hall.

Jamie stood watching everything from behind Paula's bedroom door, his heart beating faster and faster. The man came closer and closer, then suddenly Paula stopped.

Directly across from where Jamie stood was his own bedroom. Paula opened the door as quietly as she could, which was difficult because the door creaked with even the slightest movement, and stepped inside, closing the door behind her.

Jamie could hear his heart beating loud in his ears as he watched the dark figure hover outside the door with his long black cloak and dazzling white teeth. Jamie could tell he was a vampire.

The vampire waited a few moments before

disappearing through the door after Paula. Jamie stepped out from behind Paula's door into the hallway, took a deep breath, and prepared to charge.

"1,2,3," he counted, and as quick as his legs could carry him, he burst through the door!

"Aaaarrrgh!" he screamed as he ran straight into the middle of the room.

"Whoooaargh!!"

The roar of six separate voices came back at him. Jamie spun around. His dad was standing beside Paula, accompanied by a vampire, a mummy, a werewolf, and a man carrying his head under his arm. They were all laughing. Jamie took one look at them and burst out laughing himself.

Welcome to the Price family household. The Prices are no ordinary family. Ordinary families are usually scared of ghosts, but ghosts don't scare Jamie, his sister, or his father. In fact, there are certain ghosts who are more than friendly with the Prices. They're part of the family!

There's Count Vania, an unusual vampire who hates the sight of blood.

There's also Mummy, who has fascinated Jamie and his family late into the night with his tales of ancient Egypt and who amuses them even more by constantly tripping over his bandages.

Then there's Wolfie, the world's only vegetarian werewolf, who every time he catches a glimpse of himself in the mirror runs screaming from the room.

Last but not least, there's Lex Killon, an honorable old gentleman who was a passenger on the *Titanic* when it sank. Now Lex carries his head under his arm, accidentally spitting out salt water every time he opens his mouth.

Together, they are the only four ghosts that Jamie, his dad, and sister have not laid to rest. Not just because they are good friends, but because they help Jamie's dad earn a living writing horror novels.

It takes more than an ability to see ghosts to be able to write good horror stories. Jamie's dad

relies on the four friendly ghosts to give him all the information he needs about real ghosts and what makes them tick. That's what makes Andrew Price horror novels so good, because they're so real.

In fact, it's for that very reason that Jamie's dad bought their new house in the middle of the graveyard, much to Jamie and Paula's disapproval. Although they're not scared of ghosts, Jamie and Paula realized that as soon as their new classmates heard they lived in a graveyard, they would be regarded as either weird or spooky. But of course, their dad is the same as every dad—as soon as he gets something into his head, there's no getting it out again.

Whenever Jamie or Paula would tell him about their fears, he would simply smile, wink his eye and say, "Trust me," which always meant that nothing was going to go as planned.

"We nearly had you there, Jamie," said his father gleefully. By now everyone was giggling out loud.

Some, like Lex Killon, were giggling uncontrollably.

"No you didn't," replied Jamie. "I knew you were all in here. I was just trying to scare all of you first."

"Well you didn't scare me, that's for sure. I think you scared yourself more than anyone," said Paula.

Their dad agreed, "Yeah Jamie, you didn't scare me either. What about you, Count Vania?"

Count Vania floated into the middle of the room, still giggling.

"Well," he said, "there was no blood involved, so I wasn't the slightest bit scared."

"What about you, Mummy?" asked Andrew.

"No," came the muffled shout from Mummy. "It's the funniest thing I've seen in 2,000 years!"

Jamie was now getting a little frustrated. He knew he wasn't afraid but no one else in the room believed him.

"You never scared me," he said, trying to convince them, "and Mummy, if that's the funniest thing you've seen in 2,000 years, then you really should get out more often."

No sooner had the words left Jamie's mouth than the room was filled with laughter once again.

"Yeah, Mummy, you ought to get out more often!" shouted Wolfie.

"Oh really!" Mummy retorted. "Well why don't you take a look in the mirror?"

All around the room red faces were laughing hysterically.

I wish the power went out every night, thought Jamie. This is so much fun.

Outside, the wind continued to circle and swirl around the graveyard, and the rain continued to bounce hard off the windows.

Inside, Jamie and the others began making their way downstairs, their faces still red from laughing.

Suddenly, another crack of lightning lit up the graveyard to reveal a tall spooky figure standing under a tree at the end of the driveway.

It was Ebenezer Krim, the graveyard gardener.

He had been standing in the rain for some time watching the house, unable to see in because of the power outage. He stood there, not laughing or smiling, just staring.

# Be sure to check out the othe

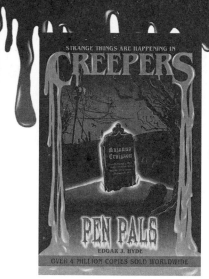

## Pen Pals
ISBN: 9781486718757

## The Scarecrow
ISBN: 9781486718788

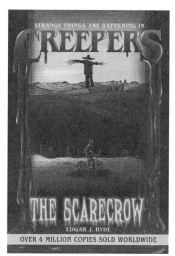

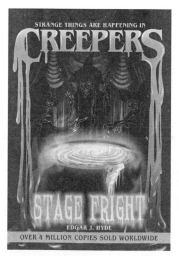

## Stage Fright
ISBN: 9781486718771